Bear's Springtime Book of Hidden Things

GERGELY DUDÁS

HARPER
An Imprint of HarperCollins*Publishers*

For my loving parents

Bear's Springtime Book of Hidden Things

For information address HarperCollins Children's Books,
a division of HarperCollins Publishers, 195 Broadway, New York, NY 10007.
www.harpercollinschildrens.com

ISBN 978-0-06-257080-2

Typography by Alison Klapthor
18 19 20 21 22 SCP 10 9 8 7 6 5 4 3 2 1
❖
First Edition

It seems like it's been winter *forever*!

Bear's ears are cold, his nose is runny, and he's sick of staying inside.

Good news, Bear: spring is here—go out and find it!

Bear starts looking for signs of spring at the farm down the road.
He's going to need a basket to collect all these springtime treasures.

Do YOU see a **basket** here?

It wouldn't be spring without a few showers.

But Bear doesn't want wet feet.

Can YOU find a **rain boot** for him?

Soon all these caterpillars will become butterflies!

But right now they look an awful lot like the little worm playing in the rain.

Where is that **worm**, anyhow?

The beautiful cherry trees are in full bloom—
what a great spot for a game of catch.
Help Bear find a **baseball** to throw around!

A breezy spring day is perfect for flying kites—

and spinning **pinwheels**!

There's one around here somewhere. . . . But where?

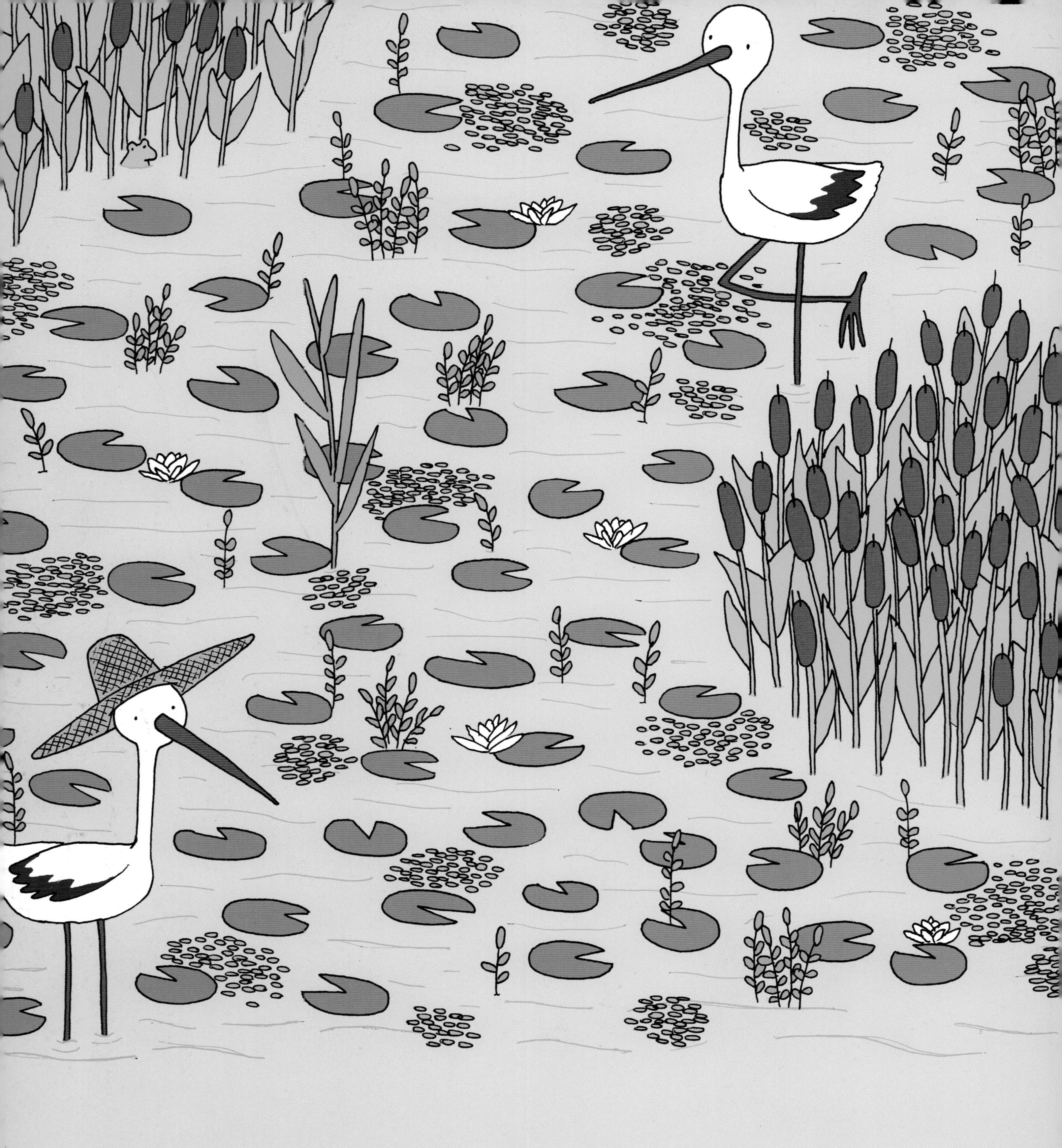

Down at the pond, Bear finds some lily pads.

Can YOU spot the **frog** hopping around?

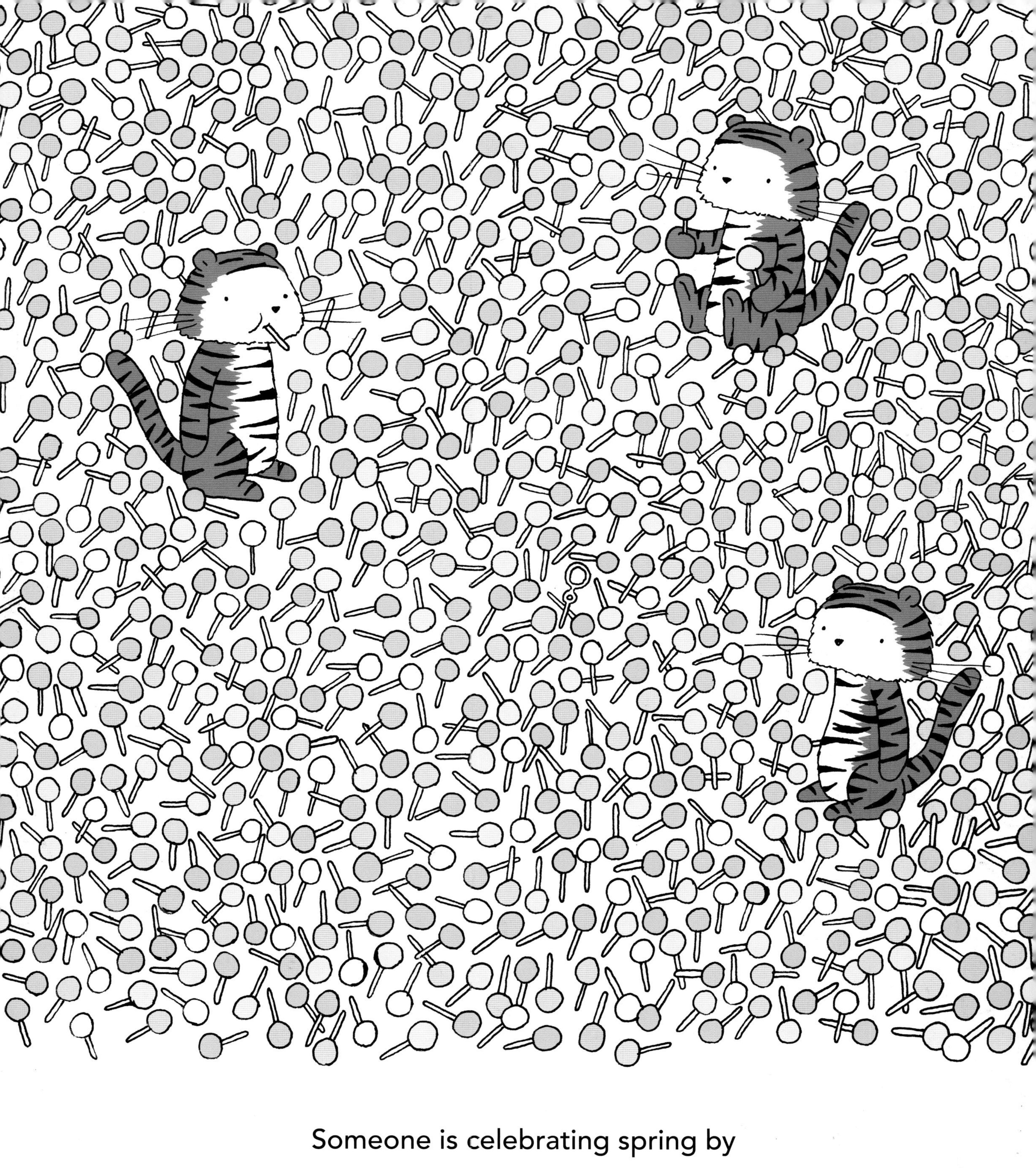

Someone is celebrating spring by
blowing bubbles with a **bubble wand**.
But the only thing the tigers want are these tasty lollipops.

Bear found plenty of spring at the farm . . .

and now he's checking if spring has arrived at the botanical garden!

Grab your **watering can**, Bear.

The brisk spring breeze has sent all these paper airplanes soaring!
And there's a single **feather** fluttering along as well.

It's time to get busy planting seeds.

Bear has plenty of flower pots—now all he needs is a **shovel**.

Buzz, buzz, buzz!

Busy bees are pollinating all the flowers.

And somewhere in there, the **queen bee**—wearing a special crown—

is the busiest of all!

The chickens are waiting for their eggs to hatch.

Can YOU spot the very first **baby chick** of the season?

The botanical garden was lots of fun.

But what has spring brought to the vegetable patch?

Bear can't wait to find out . . . just as soon as he finds a **freshly bloomed daisy**.

The vegetable patch is full of snails!

They all carry their homes on their backs . . . except one naked little slug.

Where's that **slug**?

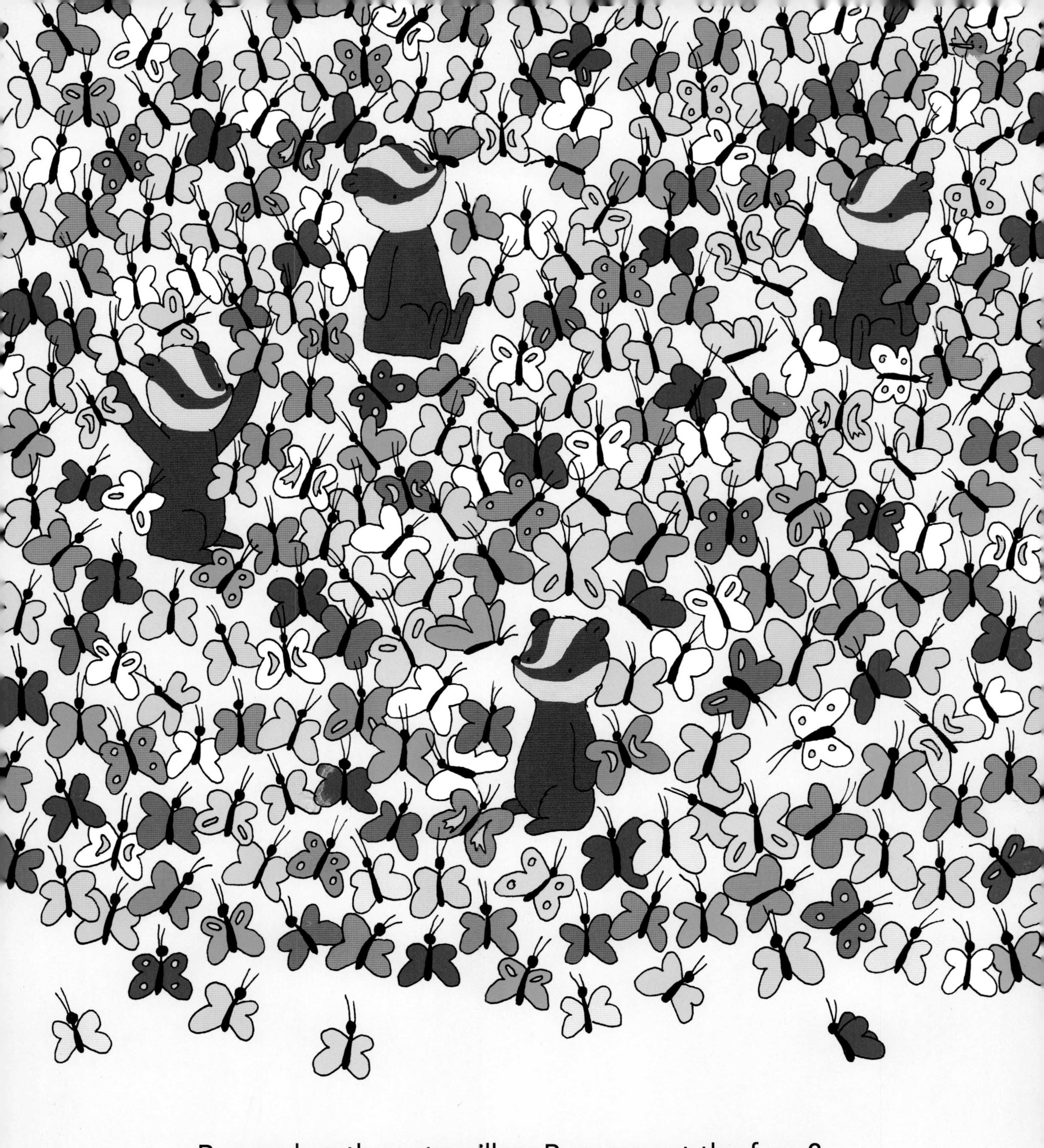

Remember the caterpillars Bear saw at the farm?

They've finally turned into butterflies!

And a jewel-colored **hummingbird** is hiding among them.

Baa, baa—quack!

There's a **duck** in this little flock of lambs.

Bear can hear it, but he can't quite see it. Can YOU?

The first blueberries of the season are just ripening.
And one very sneaky **blue jay** is determined to eat the first one.

Yes, springtime is really, truly here.
Bear's ready for a picnic in the meadow!

Can you find a **pair of cherries** for Bear to nibble?

The meadow is full of young plants just sprouting.

All that green makes it hard to find the leaf-green **grasshopper**.

Keep looking, Bear!

Grasshoppers aren't the only bugs coming to join the picnic.
There's a little red **ladybug** in all these tulips somewhere. . . .
Do YOU see her?

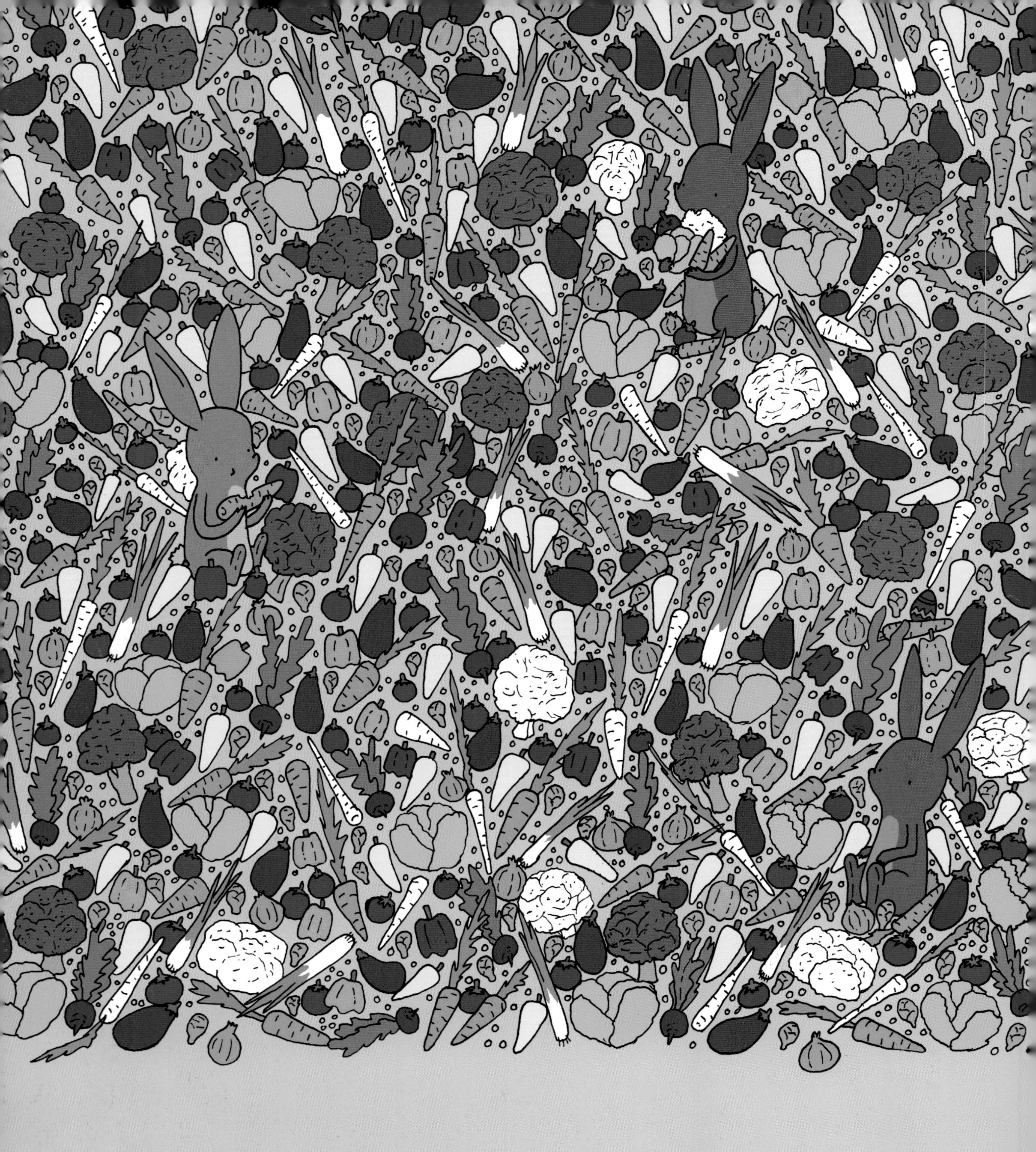

There are lots of vegetables growing in the meadow!
And someone clever has hidden a **painted egg** among them.

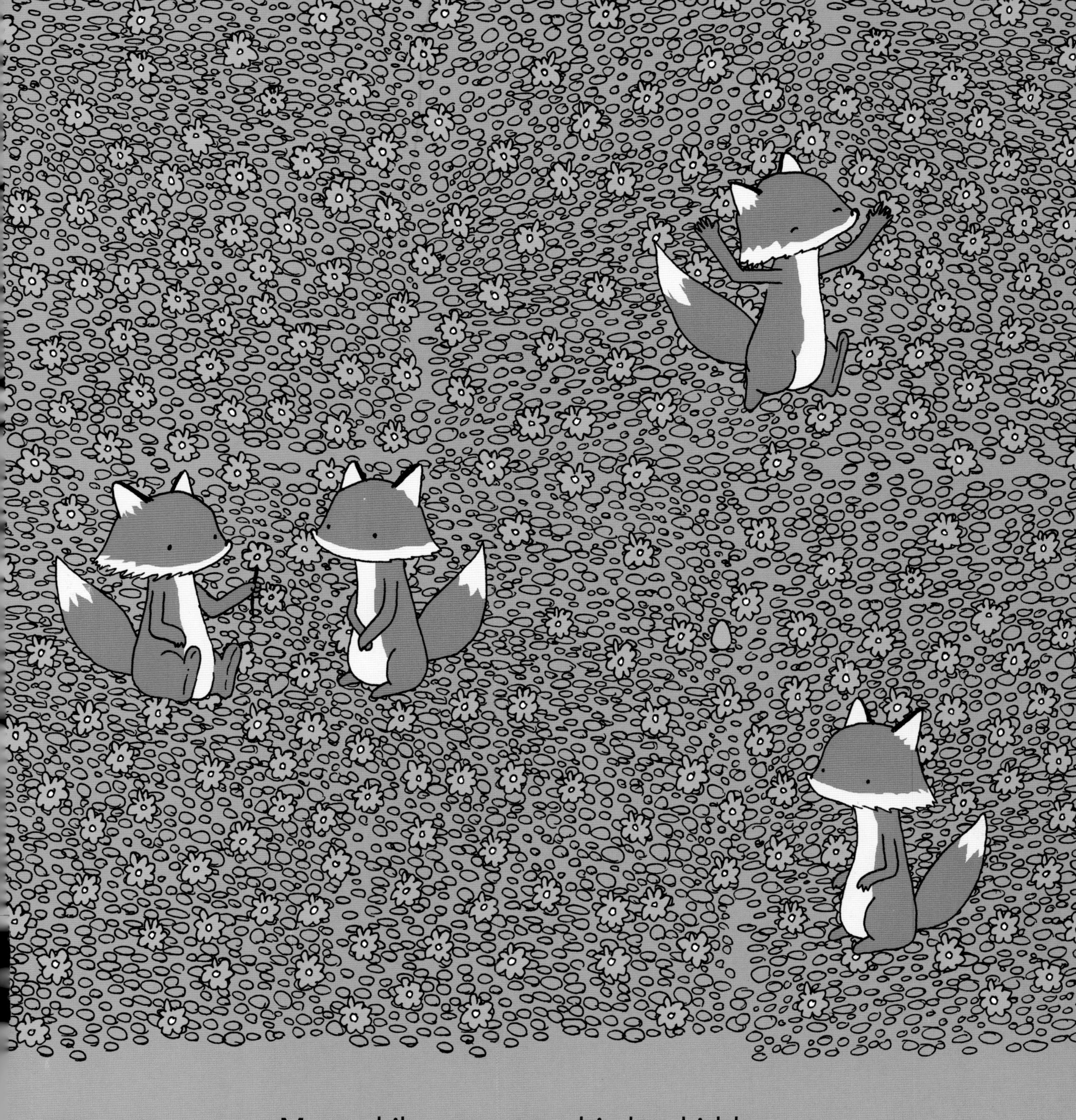

Meanwhile, a mama robin has hidden
her sky-blue **egg** in this flower bed to keep it safe,
and now she can't find it! Bear to the rescue!

Bear had a fun day welcoming in the spring.

Now it's time for a springtime party with all his friends!

Bear is so glad spring is here.

And summer will arrive before you know it!